THE FABULOUS Song

DON GILLMOR ∾ MARIE-LOUISE GAY

Stoddart Kids

TORONTO • NEW YORK

Published in 1996 by Stoddart Kids,
a division of Stoddart Publishing Co. Limited
34 Lesmill Road
Toronto, ON M3B 2T6
Tel. (416) 445-3333   Fax (416) 445-5967
E-mail Customer.Service@ccmailgw.genpub.com

Disbrituted by General Distribution Services
325 Humber College Blvd.,
Toronto, ON M9W 7C3
Tel. (416) 213-1919   Fax (416) 213-1917
E-mail Customer.Sevice@ccmailgw.genpub.com

Reprinted in September 1999

Published in the United States by Kane Miller

Canadian Cataloguing in Publication Data

Gillmor, Don
The fabulous song

ISBN 0-7737-2860-0 (bound)
ISBN 0-7737-6099-7 (pbk.)

I. Gay, Marie-Louise.   II. Title.

PS8563.I59F3 2000   jC813'.54   C95-931324-9
PZ7.G54Fa 2000

*Frederic Pipkin does his best to follow in his musical family's footsteps,
but in the end discovers his own way to express himself.*

THE CANADA COUNCIL | LE CONSEIL DES ARTS
FOR THE ARTS | DU CANADA
SINCE 1957 | DEPUIS 1957

*We acknowledge for their financial support of our publishing
program the Canada Council, the Ontario Arts Council, and
the Government of Canada through the Book Publishing
Industry Development Program (BPIDP).*

Printed and bound in Hong Kong, China by
Book Art Inc., Toronto

When Sarah Pipkin's brother was born, they named him Frederic.

"As in Frederic Chopin," Mr. Pipkin announced, "the great composer."

"Chopin was a genius," Mrs. Pipkin often added.

When the Pipkins took Frederic for walks in his
stroller, people always looked at him and said, "My,
what a beautiful baby."
"And musical, too," his mother would say.

Actually, Frederic wasn't a beautiful baby.
He looked like a turnip left too long
on the windowsill. He was
wrinkled and pale, with a tuft of
carrot-coloured hair.
He gurgled and made noises
when he ate.
To Sarah it sounded like
air leaking
out of a balloon,
but to Mr. and
Mrs. Pipkin
it sounded like a
symphony.

When Frederic was five, his parents
gave him piano lessons because Sarah had
taken them. The teacher's name was
Mr. Stricter. He lived in a dark house and
had a dog named Peanut that barked at everything.

Frederic didn't like the piano. What was worse, the
piano didn't like Frederic. When he played, it sounded
like a brick crashing through a window.

"I don't want to play the piano," he told his mother.
"You'll be glad you took lessons when you grow up,"
she said.
"Then I don't want to grow up," Frederic replied.

After three months, Mr. Stricter told the Pipkins that
Frederic would never learn to play the piano.
They bought him a clarinet.

Frederic and Mrs. Pipkin took a bus to the clarinet teacher's house. Her name was Mrs. Lumply. Frederic thought she looked like a goldfish.
When Frederic blew into his clarinet, it gave him a headache.

"You have to *feel* the music," Mrs. Lumply told Frederic. The only thing he could feel was the headache.

The best thing about the clarinet was that it was small enough to leave on the bus, which Frederic did.
When they got home, his mother noticed the clarinet was missing.
"I must have left it on the bus," Frederic said.
"By accident."
Mrs. Pipkin phoned the bus company.

The next day, Frederic and his mother drove to a warehouse that was full of all the things people leave on buses. There were sixteen clarinets, nine oboes, six saxophones, eleven cellos, twenty-nine recorders and more than a hundred violins.
Frederic saw lots of other mothers with children searching for lost instruments. Mrs. Pipkin picked out Frederic's clarinet and they went home.

Over the next few months, Frederic tried almost every instrument in the orchestra. The oboe sounded like a sick dog whining. The violin sounded like two cats fighting. He tried the saxophone, xylophone and trombone. When he blew into the trumpet, it sounded like a frog trying to spit. The banjo sounded like a frying pan hitting a frozen fence post. The cello sounded like an argument between four snakes.

Mrs. Pipkin gave Frederic a flute and stared at him hopefully. He blew into it, but no sound came out at all. Frederic went upstairs and played with his dinosaurs.

That evening, Frederic went to a concert with his parents. Sarah was playing the piano in the youth orchestra. Frederic squirmed in his chair until the conductor tapped his baton three times and the orchestra looked up at him, waiting. With one wave of the baton, the orchestra began to play. The baton leapt and swirled through the air and the music leapt and swirled with it. The conductor's hair shook as he moved, guiding the musicians. He never made a sound, but to Frederic he was amazing.

After the concert, everyone
congratulated Sarah on
her piano playing.
"You were wonderful," his mother said.
"Really great," her father said.
"You have a pimple on your nose,"
Frederic said.
"Everyone was talking about it."

On Frederic's seventh birthday, the whole
Pipkin family gathered for a huge party.
Uncles and aunts and cousins and grandparents came to
Frederic's house, and each one brought a musical instrument.
The house was full of musical Pipkins, so full that no one
could move.

The problem was, they all wanted to play a different song.
Grandpa Pipkin wanted *Happy Birthday*, Grandma Pipkin
wanted *Michael Row the Boat Ashore* and two cousins began
to play *Old MacDonald Had a Farm*. Sarah was tinkling away
at the piano and Frederic's aunt tooted *Jeepers Creepers*
on her flute.

It was more like a herd of buffalo arguing about the weather
than a birthday party.

Frederic had to do something. He climbed up on a chair and took his wooden spoon out of his pocket. He rapped it three times on his uncle's head. His uncle shouted. The room became silent as everyone stared up at Frederic in surprise.

Frederic waved the wooden spoon slowly. With his other hand, he pointed at his uncle, who began to plunk softly on his banjo. It was a song that no one had ever heard before; not even his uncle knew what he was playing.

Frederic went on waving his spoon and the oboe and guitar joined in. Then he nodded at the violin and trumpet. Soon everyone was playing the fabulous new song and wondering where it had come from.

Frederic
shook his hair
and thrashed his spoon through
the air and the musical Pipkins shook
and thrashed along with him. They played until their faces
were red, until their arms were tired, until their hearts were
pounding. They would have continued, but Frederic
lost his grip on the wooden spoon and it flew across
the room. The fabulous song ended and no one knew
where it had come from or where it had gone.

They were still wondering as they sat down at the
table. By the time dinner was served, they were arguing.
When dessert was carried in, they were all trying to
hum and whistle and sing the fabulous song. It sounded
like twelve rocket scientists talking backwards.

But Frederic wasn't listening. He had found his wooden
spoon behind the curtains and was eating his ice cream
with it. As he ate, he hummed quietly to himself. A new
song, a *stupendous* song, was playing in his head.

After dinner, the Pipkin Family Orchestra would play it.
And he, the Great Frederic Pipkin, would lead them.